Long Odds

Also by Jennifer Shapcott and published by Ginninderra Press
Aftertaste

Jennifer Shapcott

Long Odds

Acknowledgements

I would like to thank the following people who gave advice on drafts of these stories: Ann-Mari Jordens, Christine McCaffrie, Robyn Cadwallader, Di Lucas, Jenni Savigny, and Biff Ward. I would also like to thank Chris, Kyle and Lyndon for their help and support, and my publisher, Stephen Matthews of Ginninderra Press.

Long Odds
ISBN 978 1 76041 395 8
Copyright © Jennifer Shapcott 2017
Cover: Chris Brooks

First published 2017 by
GINNINDERRA PRESS
PO Box 3461 Port Adelaide 5015
www.ginninderrapress.com.au

Contents

Gratitude

Blakey planes the boat towards the point and curses Tony for sleeping in. By the time we reach the bombora, a band of gold has spread across the horizon and a breeze is ruffling the surface of the sea.

'Do you think a southerly's coming in?' I ask Blakey.

'Nah,' he replies, taking off his life jacket and flinging it into the bow. 'Nothin'll blow in till late this arvo.'

A boat zooms by heading shoreward with a man and a woman huddled over the steering wheel.

'Why are they going back then?'

'Once-a-yearers. Probably forgot to plug the bunghole,' says Tony, passing me a fishing rod.

'Maybe they freaked out when they heard the sound of barking out there,' adds Blakey.

'Barking?'

'Yeah, barking and howling…like a dog on a grave.'

I shiver. Ever since we were kids, Blakey's stories have chilled my blood.

'Tell us about the barking,' says Tony, taking off his life jacket and lighting up a cigarette.

'A bloke's fishing near the point at dawn when he hears a noise like barking,' says Barney, pausing to thread a lump of tuna on the top hook of his rod. 'Mist's hanging over the waves and he can't see a bloody thing. The barking gets louder and more frantic. Just as the mist begins to clear, there's an unholy roar. Next thing, a shark hurtles out of the water with a seal in its mouth.'

'What sort of shark?' asks Tony and waits as Blakey casts out his line.

'A white pointer. The bloke sees it once and then it's gone. And here's the weird bit: a few days later, from the top of the cliff, people spot a white mass washed up on shore. It looks a bit like a windsurfer's sail until they climb down to check it out. Turns out it's a shark with a seal stuck in its mouth.'

'The shark choked on the seal?' I ask.

'Yeah, the seal got its own back.'

I shiver again.

Blakey smiles, his eyes glinting like a boy who's hit his mark with a slingshot. 'One of youse needs to tell a story now.'

'Okay,' Tony replies. 'This one's about a stingray.'

'The one called Stumpy who hangs around the ramp?' I ask, trying to reconnect with Tony, who's been a bit distant since I announced that I was going to marry his sister, Sally.

'No, another one, twice as large, and with his tail intact. I swear this is a true story, by the way. A diver's gathering abalone in the bay. A shape passes over him, casting a shadow on the sand. The diver turns in the opposite direction but it's too late. The ray drops down and begins to wrap itself around him. The diver tries to cut the bag of abs from his waist but the ray drags him down. The man blacks out and when he comes to, he's floating on the surface and the ray's shot through with his ab bag. He backstrokes to shore and collapses on the sand. Then he laughs like a madman, he's so bloody grateful to be alive.'

'I've heard that one before,' says Blakey.

Tony shrugs and reels in his line to check the bait. 'Your turn, Simon.'

Only one story comes to mind. 'Sally and I were dining at an Italian restaurant in Manly last week. It was quiet and a bit dark, with candles flickering and casting silhouettes on the walls. Only a couple of tables were occupied. There was one with two women but somehow they didn't gel. One was older, and looked like a suburban matron; the other one had a nose ring and a purple mohawk. She treated the older woman with reverence as if she were her teacher.'

'Ya story's got nothing to do with fishin'.'

'No one said that was a prerequisite.'

'No one said that was a prerequisite,' Blakey repeats in a sing-song voice. 'Ya should hear yaself.' Menace flashes in his eyes.

'Shut up, Blakey,' snaps Tony. 'Let him finish the story.'

'The older woman gives the younger woman a gift, a parcel wrapped in silver paper with a gold ribbon. The younger woman's eyes light up. I've been staring a long time now, but I'm so curious I don't care if they notice.'

'And we don't care if ya stop now,' says Blakey, a cigarette dangling from the corner of his mouth as he struggles to release a snag in his line.

'The younger woman opens the parcel and takes out a pair of large brown mittens. She puts them on and claps. I can see the mittens magnified in a silhouette against the wall. She laughs with delight like a child who's been handed the biggest present from underneath a Christmas tree.'

'And?' asks Tony, drawing on his cigarette, impatiently.

'Well, I wondered about the gift. Did the older woman know the younger woman needed mittens for some activity, like bushwalking or skiing? Was the younger woman really pleased or was she acting? It got me thinking. That's all.'

'Not much of a story,' says Blakey, shaking his head as he recasts his line.

'It's as good as yours.'

'Nah, it's not. In my story, something happened. The shark died and we know why.'

'But there's nothing left to think about.'

'They're both bloody fantastic stories,' says Tony, opening up a slab of beer and passing each of us a stubby.

I don't tell them what occurred later that night when I gave Sally a present made by a silversmith friend. I'd shown him a photo and asked him to make a pendant to match her eyes and red hair.

'It's beautiful but I can't afford it,' I said when he showed it to me
– a sapphire embedded in a Celtic design of interwoven silver pieces.

'Pay me when you've landed a lectureship.'

When I presented the pendant to Sally, she said, 'Cool', shoved it
in her handbag and proceeded to talk about wedding arrangements.

The wind has fallen away and the sea is glassy. We catch flathead and
red rock-cod. Tony's scathing about the red rock-cod. Rubbish fish, he
calls them.

'Poor man's lobster,' says Blakey, using a glove to remove the hook
from the fish. 'They're good eatin'. Just gotta be careful with 'em.'

We catch Maori fish gleaming with rainbow colours, but mainly
we reel in red rock-cod. Blakey and Tony have drunk half the slab, and
empty bottles roll across the floor of the boat.

Somehow I catch a huge snapper with a high forehead and angry
eyes. I haul it into the boat, manage to remove the hook and throw the
fish back in the water.

'Ah nah, don't tell me, an animal liberationist is about to marry
into Tony's family,' Blakey sneers. 'What a loser.'

'You're the loser, stuck at Paperbark Bay all your life,' I reply,
winding the hook around the rod to show I've finished fishing for the
day.

Blakey puts down his bottle of beer and lets fly. 'The only reason
why Sally is marryin' ya is so she can change gears in the social stakes,
so her family can move up a notch.'

'Back off, Blakey,' says Tony. 'That's my sister you're talking about,
that's my family.'

'The great McMahon family. They can't afford a sea view in Sydney
so they build a mansion at Paperbark Bay to show off to their mates
in Penrith.'

'Why are you coming out with all this bullshit now?' asks Tony.

Blakey takes a swig of beer and looks at Tony for a few moments
before replying. 'I've heard your mum down at the sports club, braggin'

how her daughter's gonna marry into a family of judges and academics. She even thinks Simon'll be a good influence on you.'

'That's bullshit,' says Tony, his eyes narrowing.

'Why else would Sally settle for a bloke like Simon, as underdone as a piece of raw meat.'

'I've had enough. I'm getting out of here,' I say, grabbing the goggles from my backpack. I take off my life jacket and strip down to shorts and T-shirt. Then I climb over the boat and lower myself in the water.

'For God's sake, Simon,' says Tony, leaning over to pull me back in. 'Don't be so bloody stupid.'

I hesitate before swimming off. A wind has begun to blow in and the waves smash and wash over me. I'm struggling to stay afloat.

'Watch out for the rays,' laughs Blakey.

'You'll need this,' says Tony, passing my life jacket over.

'No I won't,' I reply, throwing it back into the boat. 'I'll swim underwater.'

As I set off, Blakey revs the engine like a racing car and zooms off.

I dive down and swim below the waves holding my breath for as long as I can. My heart misses a beat when a stingray passes overhead. I surface and force myself to control my breathing and dive down again. As I near the bay, the underwater world of my childhood reassures me: rock walls with sea urchins poking out of crevices, and strands of seaweed moving with the current. I reach a line of rocks and come up for air, clinging to a rock ledge for a few moments before submerging myself again. When I catch sight of a long shape hovering in an underwater cave, I tell myself that sharks are rare near the point, despite Blakey's story, and dive on.

I make it to a long flat ledge and scramble over rock pools before lowering myself into the channel of water that leads to the beach. My lungs are splitting and flashes of light dance before me but from the sound of the surf I know I'm close. I propel myself forward, tumble through the waves and somersault into shore.

I lie on the sand, my chest heaving as relief sweeps over me. When

I've caught my breath, I sit up, scan the ocean and spot a small shape vanishing into the horizon. I take off my clothes and wring them out as best I can.

The argument on the boat comes back to me, especially Blakey's words about why Sally wants to marry me. I decide to head to the McMahons' house and walk to the base of the cliff, where I scramble up a fisherman's track. As I set off, the sky darkens. Birds fall silent and the air feels cold on my skin. A wind blows in, tossing twigs and pieces of bark across the path. Lightning forks across the sky. When the thunder rolls in, rain comes down and strikes hard against my back. I decide to take shelter at the old shack near the edge of the cliff, hoping it hasn't collapsed into the sea since I was last there as a teenager.

It's still there, Jack's Burra with the painting on the outside wall – a long-eared white rabbit grinning at a fish at the end of his rod. I stumble around in the rain until I find the key hidden near the water tank. A fire is laid in the rough earthen hearth, a box of matches nearby. I strike a match, my hands shaking with exhaustion and cold. I crouch down as the flames leap up and warm me

I sit in front of the fire and turn over Blakey's words.

I loved the kaleidoscope of action in the McMahon family – surfing, snorkelling, water skiing, fishing – unlike my family, who stayed indoors reading, even when holidaying at Paperbark Bay.

Sally and I had fallen in love as teenagers exchanging kisses in the sand dunes. One night at Jack's Burra we almost went further until a sense of responsibility overcame me.

Later, my family stopped coming to Paperbark Bay. Tony worked for his father's real estate business in Penrith while I went to university in the city. Our paths seldom crossed. Sally headed off overseas, backpacking through Europe and Asia, sending me postcards with hearts over the letter 'i'.

When Tony and I had run into each other at a party in Sydney the previous year, I accepted his invitation to spend Christmas at Paperbark Bay and quickly reignited my relationship with Sally. Perhaps too quickly, I realise, as I reflect on Blakey's words, pondering the reasons why Sally and I had decided to marry.

At the sound of a helicopter flying low, I emerge from my daze. I leave the shack and make my way to the McMahons' house. A car stops and I recognise Pete, a local fisherman. He pushes the door open for me and when I climb in, he turns the ignition off.

'They're out looking for you and the others.'

He tells me about the mayday call Blakey made as the storm blew in, and later, the overturned boat with three life jackets floating nearby.

He pulls out his mobile. 'I'll let the police know you're OK. Then I'll drive you to the McMahons'.'

When Mrs McMahon opens the door, I ask if there's any news of Tony and Blakey. She shakes her head. From the expression on her face I know she fears the worst.

Sally walks into the room and looks at me as if I'm a distant relative. I go to hug her but she pulls away.

'The police just rung. They told us that you left the boat and swam to shore,' she begins, her voice as cold as the ocean depths. 'You bailed out on Tony and Blakey.'

Her eyes are hard as sapphires. I realise she will look at me like this forever.

There is no joy on the faces of the McMahon family, no gladness that I've survived. No one is clapping their hands in delight.

Secrets

A girl walked into our house one Sunday morning and sat down on the sofa as if she owned the place. Short denim skirt, fur-trimmed jacket with a hood, black stilettos. Blonde hair with one long strand hanging over her face.

'Have we met?' I asked.

'No,' she said, yawning as she flicked through a magazine on the coffee table.

'And you are?'

'Stacey. Is Sean here?'

'No. He's at soccer training.'

'OK.' She rose slowly and stretched like cat who'd taken a nap in the sun. 'I didn't realise he lived with his parents.'

'I didn't know he had a friend called Stacey.'

'See ya,' she called, tottering out, with the smell of alcohol in her wake.

I decided not to tell Sean that she'd called by. Mike was at work, as usual.

The next day on my way to Fiasco café, a motorcyclist zoomed across the pavement in front of me – a young woman wearing frayed denim shorts and a fur-trimmed jacket. Stacey.

'You almost knocked me over,' I called out.

She turned around and took off her helmet, letting out a stream of fair hair. I thought I saw a flicker of recognition pass through her eyes, but she shrugged as if we'd never met.

'You survived, didn't you?' she called out and sauntered into the café.

I noted the model of her Ducati motorbike. Taking a seat, I surveyed the café but there was no sign of her; just the usual crowd:

office workers enduring a corporate breakfast; freelancers swiping their iPads; jobseekers polishing résumés; others, like me, who'd given up and started the crossword.

Then I saw her behind the counter. She was neatly dressed in a black skirt and white T-shirt, black bra straps visible beneath. Her fringe hung over her face. It was definitely Stacey, but a neater and better organised version.

As I queued to order coffee at the counter, the man in front asked her if there were any newspapers left.

'I wouldn't have a clue,' she replied.

The tone of her voice was so offhand that people at a nearby table turned their heads. I glanced over to see if Con, the café manager, had noticed but he didn't seem to have heard.

'You're new here, aren't you?' said the man. 'Usually Con sets a newspaper aside for me.'

'Well, you'll have to ask him then, won't you?'

The man walked away, shaking his head.

When it was my turn, I placed my order and asked, 'You're not the motorcyclist who almost ran me over today?'

'Nope. Don't ride a bike,' she replied, tossing her fringe back, revealing her eyes, deep blue, the colour of love-in-the-mist flowers running wild in a garden.

'Well, it looked like you.'

'You've got the wrong person, lady.'

As she shoved me the cup of coffee across the counter, I noticed a tattoo on her right wrist – a motorbike with the word Ducati underneath.

'If you don't ride a motorbike, why do have that tattoo on your wrist?'

'Because I'm a bikie moll and I like tats. Will that do you?'

Fiasco café is big, crowded and busy. It's a good place for someone like me to sit unnoticed.

My walk to the café takes me through a street on the edge of the city. Once part of a light industrial zone, the area is now a mix of car yards, smash repair garages, boutiques and art galleries. Every day I pass a car wash where young men wash and detail luxury cars while chauffeurs and minders look on. I walk past a pub, a newsagency and a site promising a city lifestyle; in the meantime, pedestrians grumble about being pushed onto the road while the apartments are built. Skateboarders whizz past me and a young mechanic works on a car battery on the pavement near her garage workshop. The street is probably the only place in Canberra with a touch of anarchy about it. But it's safe because I won't run into former work colleagues or clients there.

I see the same faces every day: the woman who buys a Lotto ticket at the newsagency and wears a brown felt hat with an aqua feather; the man with a cane who shuffles by Fiasco café and peers into the window. I'd love to draw them, if only I could remember how.

I stay in the café until midday, when I head to Glebe Park, where office workers kick a ball on a stretch of lawn. I sit on a bench near a bed of azaleas and rhododendrons with a scent of blossom drifting through the air. I imagine that I'm still working and I'm on my lunchtime break. I try not to think about when or how I'll tell Mike I lost my job because I know the ructions it will cause in the family. In the kitchen, I make my lunch each morning as if nothing has changed.

I was thinking about Stacey as I walked over to Glebe Park on the day she'd almost run me over. It was one of those spring days in Canberra where the weather decides to turn its back on you after a run of balmy days. Rain was beginning to fall and I shivered as I stepped into the gazebo to take shelter. I had just taken out my handkerchief and wiped down the seat, when I noticed a man sitting on the opposite side. He was well-dressed in sports trousers and a jacket. Soft grey eyes, apologetic and smiling.

'A gazebo has no doors but it still makes you feel at home. Strange, isn't it?'

I nodded, my teeth chattering.

'Coffee?' he asked, holding a thermos in the air.

'You seem well prepared,' I said, accepting a cup and warming my hands around it.

'It's part of the ritual. A packed lunch and a thermos. Gets me out of the house.'

'You don't have a job?'

'I threw it in last year.'

'Any reason?'

'Hard to explain, really. Our company restructured and I ended up in the same job, the same office, I'd had ten years before. Offices and apartment buildings had sprung up and blocked the view I used to have of Mount Ainslie. When I complained and asked for a transfer, my boss suggested that I leave. So I did.'

I didn't know what to say but he went on talking anyway.

'It isn't all bad,' he said. 'There's a shortage of auditors. I'll enjoy this break, then I'll get another job. What about you? Why did you leave your job?'

'How do you know I left my job?'

'You look lost. What happened?'

I told him my story. It took longer than I'd expected.

He nodded in sympathy, then smiled and said, 'Your father strikes me as a man of principle.'

'Yes, he is. But I wish he hadn't lost me my job.'

'Surely you could have explained that it was his decision to stage a protest, not yours?'

'Yes, I could have, but in a way he pricked my conscience that day. Up till then, I'd been trying to rationalise, and cover things up for my company.'

'So what do you do now?'

'I sit in a café, rewrite my résumé and then do the crossword. What I'd really like to do is draw. I went to art school before I trained as a lawyer.'

'Sketch me.'

'I don't have anything to draw with.'

'You've got a briefcase – don't tell me you don't have a pen and paper in it.'

After I'd done a rough sketch of him, he stood up.

'I look at it this way,' he said, resuming the earlier conversation as if we hadn't stopped. 'It's a pity you got sacked, but you'll get another job. And at least your father was taking a stand on something, and so were you. Better than most ways of losing a job.'

'You think so?'

'Yes. You can tell people with pride about how your elderly father led an anti-uranium rally and marched into your law firm with a cake shaped like a yellow brick. How did he get through security, by the way?'

'He said he was my dad and had a birthday cake for me, iced in yellow, my favourite colour. Then he strode into the conference room and put the cake down in front of the firm's partners. He chuckled that it wasn't very radioactive, no more than the tailings flowing into rivers and creeks that they'd declared untainted on behalf of a mining company.'

We sat in the gazebo for a few moments longer before he began speaking again. 'You won't starve because you lost your job. For younger people, scraping by from pay day to the next, it'd be a disaster.'

After he'd left, I leaned back and closed my eyes, relieved to have told my story. There was something else; I'd been thinking about complaining to Con about Stacey. I wouldn't now.

When Con brought over my coffee, I showed him the sketch I'd done in the park.

'It's good,' he replied. 'A friend of yours?'

'Not really. More like a mentor.'

Stacey was clearing cups nearby. She stopped and scrutinised the drawing. 'Why are you using biro? Don't you have any charcoal?'

'I'm sorry. I didn't know you were an art expert.'

'I'm not. I did a course at TAFE. I wanted to be a graphic designer but I didn't finish the course.'

'Why not?'

'Mum and Dad lost their business and I needed to get work to help them out.'

'I'm sorry to hear that.'

'If you want some stuff for drawing, there's an art supply shop across the road.'

The next day I went to the shop and bought a sketchbook and charcoal.

Sean announced he wanted us to meet his girlfriend, Anastasia.

'Tell me about her,' I said.

'She graduated last year from Melbourne uni with a fine arts degree.'

'What part of Melbourne does she come from?' asked Mike.

'I don't know. She said she lived in a big house near the Yarra.'

'In Toorak or South Yarra?'

'Toorak, I think.'

'Old money. Sounds good.'

'I'd like you to meet her. Perhaps we could all go out for lunch.'

'We could have lunch here,' I suggested.

'I haven't actually told her I live with you guys.'

'What did you say she did?' asked Mike.

'She works as a volunteer curator at the National Gallery and hopes to swing a job there soon.'

Mike surprised us by suggesting that we meet Anastasia for lunch at one of the best hotels in Canberra.

'That's a bit pricey, isn't it?' I murmured.

'It tells her we have class,' replied Mike.

When Mike got into the swing of something, he'd go overboard as if paying penance for the speech nights and sports days he'd missed. He booked an oak-panelled room in a hotel overlooking the lake. Silver service and a large display of purple irises greeted us on arrival. We sat waiting, with Sean checking his watch every two minutes.

When Anastasia walked in and saw me, she seemed to falter. Then she flashed me a smile and, to my puzzlement, nodded, as if we'd entered into a conspiracy. She was wearing a cream-coloured suit, trimmed with pale pink at the collar and sleeves. Her blonde hair was tied back with a silver hair clip.

I studied her while we waited for our meal. I watched her fold and unfold her napkin. I couldn't be sure but something about the intensity of her blue eyes was making me wonder about who she really was. Her appearance and demeanour belonged to Anastasia and yet the eyes belonged to Stacey. I stared at her, searching for more evidence.

As the meal progressed, she talked about her job at the National Gallery with confidence and aplomb and I grew less sure. Either she was a first-rate con artist or I was delusional. Then I remembered something: a couple of days ago, I'd heard one of the baristas at Fiasco café complaining that Stacey was having the morning off – shopping for a new outfit, some big event coming up. Boss's niece, another muttered under his breath. That explains why she got the job, I'd almost said, but held off; Stacey had been nicer to me since I'd starting drawing.

The meal progressed with me staring at her, searching for signs. Finally, I found the clue I needed: when she spooned her crème caramel with a delicate movement of the wrist, I spotted a tattoo peeping out from the sleeve of her silk blouse.

After lunch, we wandered out to the lobby and said our farewells. When she put out her hand, I gently pushed her sleeve up and examined the tattoo – a Ducati motorbike.

'I might see you around,' I said, with a smile.

'I'm sure you will,' she said, and smiled in return, sealing our pact.

The Bowerbird

The squawking and trilling had stopped. The blue satin bowerbird had fled.

I peered into the stand of bamboo that bordered my front yard. The bower was still there, standing like a miniature tepee surrounded by blue pegs and bottle tops. But as I scanned the bamboo, I noticed something new – a construction like a shelter or a child's hut at the edge of the thicket. Sunlight flickered on green stems as I crawled towards it, squeezing my way through the bamboo until I reached a tiny clearing. In the middle of the clearing stood a small cubby made of branches interwoven with leaves, an old shirt stretched over the top. Inside lay a tin of tobacco, a box of matches and a packet of cigarette papers. I was about to hurl the tin out of the bamboo when it struck me it would be better to leave it there and see if its owner returned.

Just as I was crawling out of the bamboo, I saw a neighbour walking towards my front door. Rob used to call him the Colonel on account of his neatly pressed shorts, long white socks and polished brown shoes. Usually he pretended not to see me when I collected my newspaper from the lawn in the morning, probably an act of gallantry on his part in light of my flannelette pyjamas and gardening boots.

'Excuse me,' I called out. 'Do you want something?'

'Samantha, I don't want to alarm you,' he began, walking towards me, 'but a young lad's been hanging round your bamboo thicket.'

'Do you know who he is?' I asked, frowning with irritation that the Colonel knew my first name.

'He belongs to the house with the collection of utes parked out the front. He rides a BMX round the front yard for hours.'

'Aidan?'

'You know him?' he asked, walking towards me, staring at my boots as if inspecting me on a parade ground.

'He did some odd jobs for me earlier this year.'

'He walks into your bamboo stand in the early afternoon when he should be at school. If you see him, ring me and I'll tell him to clear out.'

'No. I'll deal with him myself,' I replied, turning away.

The Colonel took the hint and returned to his side of the street.

I went into the house, made a cup of tea and thought about Aidan. He'd turned up one day in early summer. I'd thought he was different then.

'I'm Aidan from down the street,' he said, his green eyes fixing on a spot behind me.

'Everything OK?' I asked, glancing at the BMX bike lying near the door.

He seemed taken aback as if no one had ever asked him the question. For a moment our eyes met.

'Yeah, I'm fine. I can saw 'em up for ya,' he said, pointing to some branches that had fallen down from a gum tree in the front garden.

I'd dragged them into a heap, telling myself I'd deal with them sometime – like Rob's clothes that were still hanging in the wardrobe.

'I don't have a saw. I've only got an axe.'

'It's OK,' he shrugged.

I showed him the axe and he started hacking at the wood. He wasn't a strong kid; his shoulders were narrow and he chopped awkwardly but he stuck at it and got a rhythm going. After he'd chopped four or five branches, I brought him out some lemonade. He muttered thanks without smiling. I stole a glance at him as he gulped it down, beads of perspiration clinging to the down above his lip. He came back the next day to chop more branches. Every so often, I stopped at the kitchen window to watch him, glad to have activity and movement in the backyard.

After he'd chopped up all the branches, I showed him how to weed the vegie garden. He picked it up quickly, learning to recognise the weeds from the herbs, humming as if he was enjoying his own world. When I told him that there was nothing else left to do, he shrugged and turned away as if he barely knew me. After he'd left, the place seemed still as a graveyard. Sometimes walking down the street, I saw him riding his BMX on the concrete front yard of his house. I waved at him, but he didn't wave back.

I stood up and walked round the kitchen, wondering what to do about him smoking in the bamboo grove. I kept thinking how Rob would have known what to do. A year since his death and I still expected him to sit down at the table and talk with me.

I'd tracked the bowerbird since the start of spring, when he'd flown into the garden in flash of glossy blue feathers. He'd staked out his territory, carrying pegs and buttons in his beak and depositing them around my garden. After he'd scattered bright objects everywhere, he hopped into the bamboo grove, wearing a track between the stems. He patrolled the entrance, hissing and screeching if other birds approached. One day I peered into the bamboo and saw a bower made from twigs. Blue pegs and bottle tops, shiny buttons, glass stones, a lapis lazuli earring, feathers from crimson rosellas and pieces of string, lay scattered around it. Now he was gone, the garden stood lifeless and still.

I decided to take an afternoon off work and tell Aidan to stop smoking in the bamboo.

I waited in the front room, peering through the blinds every five minutes. It wasn't long before I spotted someone approach the front garden and enter the bamboo thicket. Slight build, sandy-coloured hair, a determined walk. Aidan.

I walked outside and crawled into the bamboo. He was sitting in his hut, rocking backwards and forwards.

'What are you doing here, Aidan?'

He stopped singing and took out his earphones, staring into the distance before speaking. 'Just listenin' to music on me phone.'

'Why do you have to come into the bamboo to do it?'

He shrugged. I waited for him to speak again but he sat staring at a point behind me as if I'd gone away.

'You've got a home, haven't you?' I asked.

'I get a bit of peace here.'

'You've upset the bowerbird. If you want to smoke, go behind the woodshed in my backyard and do it.'

So that's how it started, Aidan leaning against my woodshed in the early afternoons, a rollie stuck on his lip as he rocked back and forth to music on his phone. After an hour or so, he'd hide his tin of tobacco behind the wood box and set off home. I knew he shouldn't wag school, knew he shouldn't smoke, but I told myself the whole world was probably nagging and lecturing him, so why should I join the queue. And if he smoked behind my woodshed, and stayed out of the bamboo thicket, the bowerbird might come back.

A few weeks later, I heard buzzing and trilling in the front garden. The bowerbird was back. He'd returned with new sounds too: clicking and whirring noises as if he'd spent time near machines. I smiled at the thought of him finding a patch of bamboo or wild fennel near a factory, maybe feeding off lunchtime scraps from workers. I wondered what had brought him back to my front yard; perhaps his treasure trove around the bower or the green sanctuary of the bamboo grove. Somehow he'd known it was safe to return.

When I set off to work the next day, I glanced in the direction of the bamboo, happy to hear his chirpings, glad to know he'd be there on my return.

With Aidan in the backyard and the bowerbird in the bamboo, I thought I'd sorted things out, but one day when I was picking up the newspaper from the lawn, the Colonel strode across the road and shattered my peace.

'That young lad, I saw him walk into your garden the other day,' he said, drawing himself up so much he towered over me. 'I followed him to see what he was up to. He had headphones on and didn't notice me. I saw him open the gate to your backyard and roll a cigarette.'

'I told him he could smoke there. That way he doesn't scare the bowerbird.'

'He's wagging school and smoking. You need to talk to his parents. If you don't, I will.'

I flinched. 'No. Don't tell his parents.'

'I have no choice. Everything's tinder-dry at the moment. He'll set your house on fire.'

'I'll talk to him.'

As soon as I came home from work that day, I went round to the backyard. Aidan was leaning against the shed, rolling a cigarette.

'It's a problem you're smoking here,' I said.

'How come?'

'Well, for a start, your parents don't know about it.'

'If you tell me parents about me smokin' –'

'What?'

'Nuthin'.'

'I won't tell them but can you please stop smoking here.'

He shrugged and lit up the cigarette.

'You can still come here and listen to music, just don't smoke.'

'If you tell me parents –' he began and stopped.

'What? What will happen?'

He shrugged again and looked away. I knew he wasn't going to stop smoking. I would have to talk to his parents before the Colonel did. I began to walk down the street but something stopped me – the image of him leaning against the woodshed, eyes closed, clinging to a small moment of peace. I turned and walked back to my house.

Three days later, I came home to see a plume of smoke rising from the bamboo. I grabbed a hose but the flames crackled and leapt through the thicket. My hands shook as I phoned the fire brigade; all I could think about was whether the bowerbird had managed to escape. By the time the fire brigade arrived, the flames were racing across the front garden. The firies put out the fire but the bamboo grove was reduced to a patch of blackened stalks. I raked over the ashes and a few twisted pieces of blackened plastic pegs where the bower had once stood. There was no sign of the bowerbird.

The next morning, the Colonel told me he'd seen Aidan near the bamboo thicket. 'I bet he lit the fire. He was probably angry because his parents found out he'd been smoking behind your woodshed.'

'And he thinks I told them,' I said, turning away.

I walked down to Aidan's house and knocked on the door. I wanted to tell him I hadn't dobbed him in. No one answered the door, that day or the next.

In the following months, whenever I walked past his house, I expected to see him riding his BMX but there was no sign of anyone in the front yard.

One morning, the Colonel crossed the road to tell me Aidan had gone up north to his grandfather's place. I shrugged and didn't say anything. We went back to ignoring each other in the mornings.

After the late spring rain, the bamboo sprang shoots of soft green. There was still no sign of the bowerbird but in early summer I heard squawking in the backyard. I smiled when I looked out the window and saw him trilling and chirping as he surveyed his new domain from the branch of a plum tree. When he flew off, I searched the backyard for his bower. Peering below the arch of raspberry canes, I spotted a tiny structure of twigs surrounded by pegs, bottle tops and faded snail shells.

Over summer I watched him dart in and out of the raspberry canes, carrying more objects in his mouth. Soon an olive-green female bowerbird turned up and the backyard buzzed with chatter.

One day, I knelt down to see what was happening under the raspberry canes. I glimpsed the male bowerbird moving around the bower, lowering himself in front of the entrance, jigging and dancing to impress her.

For days, the two birds hopped around the raspberry bushes and into the canes to cavort around the bower.

A few weeks later, I saw them flying out of my back garden, carrying twigs to build a nest. I looked around the trees in the street but couldn't spot it. I guessed they'd built high in the trees, out of sight.

When they left my backyard at the end of summer, I missed their sounds but the sense of loneliness wasn't the same as when the bowerbird decamped the first time. This time it was more like a couple of noisy visitors who'd left with a promise to return next year.

The bamboo in the front yard grew back thick and green but something haunted me whenever I looked at it. I couldn't get the memory of the flames out of my head, bursting through the grove like a surge of anger. I hoped that one day Aidan would realise that I hadn't betrayed him. I hoped he'd come back again.

First Day Out

'Why's Johnno parked outside with his boat and ute?' asked Yvonne as soon as she walked in the door.

'Because he knows better than to come inside,' I replied, giving her a quick peck on the cheek.

'You're not supposed to mix with the old crowd.'

'I've waited five years to go fishing.'

'Your parole officer said to phone first thing today.'

'I'll ring him when I get back,' I replied, heading out the door.

'Check the glovebox,' said Johnno when I climbed in. 'Royce has given ya a welcome home present.'

'I'm clean these days.'

'It's good gear. Ya can always move it.' He reached over to the glovebox and threw a packet in my lap.

I threw it back and slammed the glovebox shut.

The ute bumped along the track to the beach and the sun rose like a ball of orange above the paperbark trees.

When we reached the estuary, it was as if I'd never been away – pelicans circling over the river; the smell of salt in the air; surf thundering behind the dunes.

'It's bloody bright,' I said, raising my hand against the glare.

'Should've got here first light. What kept ya?'

I didn't answer straight away. I was watching a woman with a mop and metal bucket lumber towards the toilet block near the jetty. Hair flecked with grey tied back in a ponytail. I thought of what Yvonne had told me last night how she'd rather leave town and clean toilets than have me work for Royce again.

'I had to wait till Yvonne finished her night shift at the hospital.'

'Royce wants to talk to ya.'

'To find out whether I blabbed inside?"

'He knows ya didn't squeal on him. He's got a plan. Ya gotta talk to 'im.'

'I thought you and I were going fishing, not catching up with Royce.'

Neither of us spoke as we crossed the bar, the boat rising and thumping against the swell. We fished for an hour, with Johnno doing most of the reeling in. An albatross flew overhead, wings stretched wide as it dropped down and floated over us, close enough to touch, moving on when it saw there was no catch on our lines.

The fish seemed to know I'd lost the knack. I'd get a bite but not strike in time. Every time I reeled in, the bait was gone, the hook empty.

'Jeez, Pete, ya running through me bait,' Johnno sighed every time he opened the tackle box.

Eventually I landed a red rock-cod. When I took it off the hook, my thumb got caught on one of the spikes. Pain shot up my arm like a bolt of electricity.

'Told ya to wear a glove,' said Johnno. 'Are ya goin' to rebait or what?'

'Think I'll leave it for a bit,' I replied, nursing my arm.

'The swell's settled. Might try the point,' said Johnno, reeling in. He revved the engine hard and planed the boat towards the point.

A line of haze stretched across the horizon, reminding me of the vastness and space I'd missed while I was away.

As we neared the point, Johnno slowed the boat and ran it close to shore, skimming past rock ledges and coves with overhangs, places I used to hide with my abalone catch if I spotted a fishing inspector's boat.

A yacht was floating near the point, the white sails limp, waiting for a breeze. A man's silhouette clear against the sky. Lean and tall. A shiver ran through me.

'Is that Royce?' I asked.

'Yeah, he'll talk to ya at the ramp about his plan.'

'Which is?'

'He's branched out. Got out of abalones. No one could scrape 'em off the rocks quick enough. He swore when ya got sent away.'

'Should've got a better cockatoo if I was worth that much.'

'Ya shouldn't have drawn a knife on that local busybody.'

'I'd come up the cliff and seen you wrestling with someone. I thought he was a stand-over man.'

'I didn't think they'd send ya away for so long.'

My eyes ached from the brightness of the sea and the sky. My chest tightened as the boat ramp came into view.

'Ya feelin' all right?' Johnno asked.

'Yeah,' I replied, thinking about what Yvonne had said the night before, how I owed Royce nothing, how we needed to make a clean start.

'Take a look around you, Yvonne,' I'd told her, pointing to the furniture in the unit. 'We wouldn't have this if it hadn't been for Royce.'

'Loyal as a stupid mutt,' she'd said. 'We need to get away from him, make a new start.'

'Where? How?'

'We could go north to Mum's, stay with her till you find your feet.'

'What would we live off?'

'We'd find something. What about that course you did inside? Mum knows someone who needs a bookkeeper.'

'I don't want to work in an office.'

We fished at the point for a couple of hours. When we had enough for a feed, we set off back to the boat ramp.

Johnno slowed the engine as if he had something to say. 'Royce is bringing in his yacht. We can talk to him at the boat ramp.'

I thought about Yvonne's words the night before, how we owed Royce nothing.

'Are ya listenin' to me?' Johnno was saying as if I was still in a dream. 'Ya gotta talk to Royce.'

'So this morning wasn't about fishing?'

I held the rope, warm water lapping round my ankles while Johnno backed the trailer down the ramp to drag the boat out. People chatted; a few looked me up and down, maybe my pale face and crew-cut stood out. Some recognised me, most didn't. There were newcomers at the point, Johnno reckoned, retirees, and cashed-up tradies, even a few charter boats where the passengers pretended they'd caught the catch, he joked with a hollow laugh.

I looked across at a young shirtless bloke steering a boat towards the jetty, helping an older man in slacks and sports jacket climb out of the boat onto shore. The older bloke started chatting to me about the catch as if he'd hauled it in.

Johnno was right. Things were changing. I could do that, I thought, take someone out on a chartered boat, catch the fish and let someone pass it off as their own. I caught a glimpse of normality, like a soldier slipping back into civvies and walking down the street.

I hauled the esky out of the boat and began scaling the fish over the wooden deck of the jetty. A group of pelicans flew in, dropping webbed feet down like the wheels of a plane, as they skidded and landed on the water. Two of them flew up to the railing and when I'd finished cleaning the fish, one flew down and scooped up a trail of guts.

Johnno joined me at the jetty. 'Why ya keeping the heads?'

'I don't like throwing bones with spikes into the water. There's kids around.'

He shook his head as if he didn't know me. 'Even when they're dead, the red rockies jab ya,' he said after brushing his finger against a spike. He shook his hand and flinched before throwing another fish head into the water.

A pelican swooped down from the railing and swallowed the fish head in a single gulp. Seconds later, it began to shudder as the head lodged in its throat. It turned in circles, rose and sank back onto the water, its neck quivering as the poison spread, the fish head stuck sideways like a brick lodged in its throat.

I turned away and saw the shadow to one side of me. I looked up to see a pair of black polished shoes and sports trousers with neatly ironed creases in the middle.

Johnno stood up and stuck out a hand.

'I'd rather not get the smell of fish on me,' said Royce.

Johnno stood back as Royce turned to me. I rose and we faced each other, neither putting out a hand. The face as I remembered it, the high aquiline nose, the silver hair and pale blue eyes, a jumper draped over his shoulders.

'How are you settling back in?'

I looked away without answering and saw the pelican turning in circles, the shape of the fish head still visible in its neck.

Royce followed the gaze of my eyes. His eyes rested on the bird as he went on talking. 'I've started some new ventures. I've got something in mind for you.'

'I'm not allowed to keep company with past associates, part of my parole conditions.'

'We're not associates, we're as good as family,' he replied, placing a hand on my shoulder.

His eyes narrowed as I pushed his hand away and stepped away. I braced myself as he took a step towards me. He stopped and looked down the jetty. I turned to see a woman walking towards us. It was the woman with the bucket and mop, hanging round around after cleaning the toilets, waiting for the fishermen to bring in their catch.

'Ya catch much?' she called out.

'Just a few red rockies,' I replied.

'Not enough to share,' Johnno called out.

The woman kept on shuffling down the jetty towards us. I glimpsed her face worn and lined, two front teeth missing.

I thought of Yvonne the night before getting ready for work, pulling her blonde hair back and fastening it with a clasp shaped like a butterfly, and what she'd said – how she'd rather clean toilets than have me go back inside. But I didn't want her to look like this woman. I couldn't bear the idea that she would suffer for me.

'Royce's talking to you,' said Johnno. 'Answer him.'

The woman with the bucket and mop was standing a few feet away as if waiting for something to unfold. She stared at me. I looked at her lined and creased face and saw something I hadn't expected. Her eyes burned with a magnificent brightness.

I glanced cross at the pelican swimming in circles, still shaking. Maybe it would survive, maybe not. As long as it lived, there was hope. Yvonne and I could move town and start again somewhere, somehow.

I took my sunglasses off and turned to face Royce, the light from the estuary dazzling me. I stared at him, blinking into the whiteness. 'I don't want a job with you.'

'If you walk away now,' said Royce, signalling to Johnno to block my path, 'you won't be able to walk around this town. There'll be no work for you – or anyone else in your family.'

'Then I'll start again somewhere else.'

'Word spreads,' replied Royce, moving away from the jetty rail and walking towards me. 'People'll soon find out who you are, how you pulled a knife on a local who caught you poaching abalones.' He took a step closer and squared off against me then jabbed me in the chest. 'Walk away now and it's too late.'

I picked up the fish I'd gutted, placed some in a bucket and gave the bucket to the woman. She nodded and walked away.

I packed the rest into Johnno's esky. 'Take them,' I said to Johnno.

He looked at Royce, who was leaning against the jetty railing, arms crossed, eyes fixed on me.

'What about ya share?' asked Johnno, glancing again at Royce.

'I didn't catch much.'

'Wait. I'll run ya back home.'

'I'll make my own way.' I turned, walked down the jetty and took the path home.

The Reader of Riversleigh

At the sound of footsteps, I broke off from staring at the stars. 'Who is it?' I yelled as torchlight swept over the windows.

'It's Laura, from Riversleigh, the house on the hill.'

I opened the front door to find a woman who looked as if she'd stepped out of another century – barefoot, a long white nightdress, black hair piled high on her head.

'The power's gone,' she began, wrapping a shawl around her shoulders. She spoke so softly I could hardly hear her. 'I need help to change the fuses.'

'Can't it wait till morning?'

'My husband needs electricity for his medical equipment.'

I followed her down the path to where an old Mercedes was parked near a strand of casuarinas. She walked with a light step, her slender frame silhouetted in the torchlight. I half expected her to ask me to drive but she gestured to me to climb in the passenger side and walked round to the driver's seat. We drove in silence, the eyes of animals glowing as we made our way along a narrow dirt road. She edged the car down a driveway over-arched with cedar trees, parked down the side of a two-storeyed house and pointed her torch towards the fuse box.

'I haven't seen these for years,' I said when I lifted the lid and saw a line of white porcelain fuses. 'You need to put in circuit breakers.'

'My husband doesn't like tradesmen coming to the house. I'm sorry to have hauled you out. I don't even know your name.'

'Harry Taylor,' I replied, threading the fuse wire.

As soon as I changed the last fuse, the sound of opera surged from the house like a clap of thunder.

'Donald will be happy to have his Wagner back,' said Laura. 'Will you come inside so he can thank you?'

'I need to get back home. I've got a deadline tomorrow.'

'It'll only take a minute.'

We walked down a darkened hall with a soft light pulsing from a room at the end.

'Did I miss a fuse?' I asked.

'No. Donald prefers candles in his bedroom.'

Laura led me into the room where a man lay in bed, his skin as white as alabaster, black eyes glaring from deep sockets. At the foot of the bed stood an oxygen tank. I must have reacted or recoiled because when she spoke it was as if she needed to explain something.

'There's nothing that can be done for him,' she said, walking over to a stereo player and turning the music down.

'Don't talk about me as if I'm not here,' hissed Donald.

My eyes scanned the room, taking in the glow of embers in the fireplace, the shadows flickering on the walls, the velvet dressing gown draped across a chair.

'What are you staring at?' rasped Donald. 'Who are you?'

'I'm Harry, from the cottage near the mangrove island.'

'You're staring at the shadows. It reminds you of Juliet's tomb?'

I shook my head and glanced across at Laura, who ushered me out of the room.

'Shouldn't he be in hospital?' I asked as she drove me back home.

'No. He doesn't want to leave Riversleigh, not while he still has his voice.'

I held back from asking what she meant. Neither of us spoke as the car pushed its way through the undergrowth until we approached the clearing near the shack.

'Will you come again?' she asked. 'Will you read to him?'

'Read what?'

'Poems, and plays – the ones he's acted in. He's tired of my voice. He wants someone else to read to him.'

'I'm not sure I can spare the time,' I replied, shuffling in my seat.

'Thank you for tonight,' she called as I climbed out of the car.

'It was nothing.'

I didn't want to get involved with people in the valley. I'd come there to forget Helen's words: I was a drifter; unable to make important decisions, like whether to marry, or to have children. You weigh things up too much, she'd said, flinging the words at me the day I left. You understand the moral dimensions of an issue but you can't make a decision.

A few days after my visit to Riversleigh, I came across Laura again. I was wandering along the remnants of a sandstone road built by convicts, a place of lost hope with tank stands covered in blackberries and weeds growing up in the ruins of cottages. I heard the sound of sobbing and glimpsed Laura leaning against a gum tree. I was about to turn away but it was too late. She wiped her eyes and walked towards me, wrapping the ends of her shawl round her wrists.

'Would you walk with me back to Riversleigh?' she asked, smiling as if nothing was wrong.

I nodded and we followed the path until we reached the river.

'Have you lived at Riversleigh long?' I asked.

'A few years,' she said, staring at a crane that had alighted on a tree, its wings outstretched like a piece of origami unfolding. 'Donald came back here after he was diagnosed with motor neurone disease. Riversleigh was his family's country home.'

'How long…' I began.

'…does he have to live? I don't know. His body is shutting down. His voice will be the next to go.'

'There are devices he could use to get round that.'

She stared at me with disbelief in her grey-blue eyes. 'He's an actor. He's lived by his voice.'

'He could use an eye-controlled computer to type his words onto a screen.'

'He would abhor such a thing. He would rather…' She stopped talking and began walking ahead of me.

'I'm sorry,' I called out to her. 'I was thinking of ways to help… if I can.'

'Come to Riversleigh,' she said, turning round to face me. 'And read to Donald.'

I thought of Donald's irritation if I stumbled over a word, but her eyes pleaded and I relented.

'Come tomorrow morning,' she said. 'I'll make sure he's ready for you.'

Laura was working in the front garden when I arrived at Riversleigh the next day. 'Donald's in the library,' she called out.

I wanted to stop and talk but she looked away and began pruning a rose bush that straggled over a wrought-iron gate. I entered the house and walked down the hall, checking each room until I reached one filled with books on shelves that reached the ceiling.

Donald sat in his wheelchair near the window. 'Come, Harry, come in,' he whispered. 'Open the curtains and choose a book.' He pointed to a set of crimson curtains that looked as if they belonged to a stage set. 'Poetry is on the left,' he said, his voice rising a little. 'Nineteenth-century novels are in the middle. Modern on the right.'

I selected a leather-bound volume of poems by Shelley, whom I remembered studying at school. He motioned me towards the French doors and I pushed him in a wheelchair onto the terrace. Beyond lay a sweep of empty paddocks with broken fences. Stillness lay all around, broken by the occasional chime of a bellbird.

I opened the book and began reading the poem 'Ozymandias'.

'Speak up, man,' he ordered. 'Lift those broad shoulders. Project your voice to match your frame.'

I pushed my shoulders back and took a breath. When I reached the lines, 'Nothing beside remains. Round the decay / Of that colossal wreck, boundless and bare / The lone and level sands stretch far away', he joined in and recited the lines with me, his breath shortening with the effort.

I waited before continuing with another poem. 'Do you want me to go on reading?'

'No, you can go now,' he said. He closed his eyes as if exhausted by the effort.

I found Laura still working in the front garden.

'I scratched myself gardening,' she said when she saw me staring at the scars on her wrist. 'Thank you for reading to him,' she said, wrapping the shawls around her wrists.

'If he needs to go to hospital suddenly…' I said, writing down my mobile number on a piece of paper.

'He won't go to hospital,' she replied, shaking her head. 'You'll come and read to him again?'

That evening I lay awake watching a nighthawk sweep back and forth across the sky. I thought about Laura's wrists and the way she'd twisted her shawl over her forearms to hide them.

At Riversleigh the next morning, Donald gestured towards a pile of books on the outdoor table. 'The plays I've performed in. Choose one,' he said.

I chose a play by Tennessee Williams, *Orpheus Descending*, and began reading. I read from the play every day over several weeks. Donald spoke little, occasionally suggesting improvements in my delivery, sometimes smiling in anticipation of certain passages.

Most mornings, Laura worked in the garden. Sometimes he rang a bell for her to make coffee. I studied her as she poured the coffee, trying without success to glimpse the wrists wrapped beneath her shawl.

One day I tried to draw her into conversation about what she'd done before coming to Riversleigh. When she mentioned she'd worked at a theatre in Sydney, I asked what sort of work she'd done.

'Nothing worth talking about,' she said, shaking her head a little. 'Just bits and pieces to help Donald.'

'Since our marriage, Laura's greatest achievement has been to look after me,' said Donald, smiling, his face a mixture of triumph and satisfaction.

I glanced across at Laura to judge her reaction. Her face remained expressionless. It flashed through my mind that I would never get to know her. I decided to spend less time at Riversleigh.

'I won't be able to come for a few days,' I said when she walked with me to the front door. 'I've got a project to finish.'

'Don't stay away too long – please. When you read to him, it brings him to life.'

She rang me several evenings later. 'His voice is disappearing. Can you come and read to him?'

I imagined her standing at the phone table, wrapping her shawl around her wrists, candlelight flickering from the room at the end of the hall. I agreed to come the next day.

When I returned to Riversleigh, Donald greeted me in his wheelchair on the terrace. For once there were no books lying on the table.

'Do you want me to choose something from the library?' I asked.

'No,' he whispered. 'I want to talk about Laura.' His head was drooping, his breathing laboured as he fought to get the words out. 'It's her turn now.'

'What do you mean?'

'She's given me the best years of her life.' He paused again and lifted his head. His voice was reducing to a rasp. 'I want you to wheel me to the ridge near the old convict track and push me over the edge. They'll never find me in the gully. The crows can pick at me till there's nothing left but my bones.' He stared at me, waiting for my reply, frowning as if I was taking an eternity.

'But they'll look for you everywhere,' I said, and stopped, knowing my reply was inadequate, knowing I'd dodged the main issue, just as Helen always accused me of doing. 'There'll be an inquest. Laura and I would be asked to give evidence.'

'They won't find me at the bottom of the gully.'

I imagined myself pushing his wheelchair through the bush, branches poking in my face as I made my way to the top of the ridge, and when I reached it, pushing the chair over the side, sending Donald tumbling, the wheelchair smashing to pieces as it hit the ground. I saw myself walking with Laura along the river.

The chime of a bellbird tore me from my dreams.

'I'm sorry, I can't help you,' I said, shrugging as if he'd asked me for a light for a cigarette. I paused, disgusted at the inadequacy of my response and added, 'I don't know you.'

'So if you knew me better, you'd help me?' he asked, his voice hoarsening.

'It's not just about knowing someone. It's such a big thing, but the way you ask me, to take you to the gully and push you over the ridge, just like that.'

'You don't believe in euthanasia?'

'It depends on the circumstances. I'd want to think about it.'

'Then go and think about it.' He sat up, his gaze impatient. 'Go, go now…and don't tell Laura what I asked you to do.'

I spent the night weighing up whether to tell her. I decided to talk to her but when she greeted me at the front door, she spoke first.

'He wants you to take him out canoeing on the river. There's a kayak in the shed. Will you take him out on it?'

'Is he OK to sit in the canoe?'

'Yes, but you'll need to lift him in.'

I hauled the kayak with its faded canvas cover down to the river while Laura pushed Donald in his wheelchair at a distance behind me.

No one had used the jetty at Riversleigh for a long time. Water reeds poked through gaps in the wood; a few streaks of white paint clung to the pylons.

I lifted Donald out of his wheelchair and lowered him into the back seat of the canoe.

'Paddle down to the mangrove island,' he whispered. 'Take me to where the roots of a fallen tree stick out of the water.'

I dipped the paddle into the water, glancing behind at him between strokes, fearful he might fall into the water.

The tide was flowing fast when we reached the bend where the roots of an upturned gum tree rose out of the water.

'Stop here,' he ordered, his voice barely audible.

I turned to face him, my chest tightening.

'Turn around fully towards me,' he said. 'Then push me into the water.'

'No,' I said, laying down the paddle. 'Donald, you need to talk to someone about things…a counsellor, a professional.'

'I need to bring this to an end,' he rasped. 'Push me into the water. Do it now.'

We stared at each other. I thought of Laura and her freedom.

'Do it.' His face looked more animated than I'd ever seen it, as if the act he was contemplating had infused him with energy.

I looked away, trying to work out what to say. Swifts were flying over water, picking off insects. A shaft of light illuminated the dappled bark of the gum trees lining the banks of the river and the tips of the burrawang ferns glinted in the sun.

'You're still alive,' I said.

'You don't have the guts to do it,' he whispered.

'It's not my choice to make.' I picked up the paddle and turned the canoe around.

Laura was waiting at the jetty. Donald's wheelchair bounced up and down as she pushed him along the track back to the house. His face had frozen into a grim unsmiling mask.

When we reached Riversleigh, he took out a handkerchief and raised his hand in an attempt to wipe his brow. Laura and I stood waiting. Finally, his hand dropped to his lap. His fingers clenched the handkerchief in a tight ball. Laura opened the door and wheeled him into the house. I waited outside. When she came back some time later, I took her hand and raised it to my face.

Just before dawn, I woke to the smell of gum trees burning. When I stepped outside, I saw a plume of smoke rising from the direction of Riversleigh. I tore through the bush, my heart pounding in my ears. By the time I reached the last rise on the track, flames were soaring from the roof of Riversleigh, licking the sky; windows began to explode, sending shards of glass across the lawn.

I was halfway down the drive when I spotted Laura in the front garden. I ran towards her.

'Last night Donald's voice disappeared completely,' she whispered, drawing her shawl around her shoulders.

'Where is he?' I yelled. 'Which room?'

'He told me he wouldn't suffer this way. He'll suffocate from smoke inhalation before the flames reach him.'

I ran into the house, the smoke filling my lungs and choking me as I struggled down the hall. I grabbed a towel from the kitchen, dampened it, and covered my face. When I entered the bedroom, I stepped back. The curtains were on fire and the flames were spreading across the room. Donald lay on the bed, his face at peace as the fire danced towards him. He didn't respond when I lifted him up and carried him down the hall.

'Why? Why, are you doing this?' asked Laura, when I staggered out of the house with Donald in my arms.

'Because I can't let him die,' I replied, gasping for air.

She stood beside me as I placed my hands on his chest and began to resuscitate him. 'Then it would have been better if you'd never come to Riversleigh.'

I brought Donald back to life but he died a few days later.

For months after the fire, people came to see the blackened ruins of Riversleigh. Laura went back to Sydney.

Sometimes when I watched the stars rise in the evening sky, I let my mind play out a scene: I hadn't rushed into the house to save Donald; I'd stood with Laura and watched Riversleigh burn. We'd started a new life together. It took a long time to force myself out of my imaginings.

Long Odds

'Hi, Adrianna, I'm at the airport. I'll send you a text when I get to London. Love, Mum.'

Adrianna curled the coils of the handset around her finger for some time before phoning her sister and brother.

'Damn. I was hoping she'd babysit this weekend,' said Susan.

Her brother James hadn't known his mother was going to London either. 'That's the third trip this year. Maybe she's caught up in a romance scam. I'd better check her bank accounts.'

'How will you do that?' asked Adrianna.

'I help her with her finances. I know all the passwords.'

'Tell me if you find anything,' she replied. But you won't, she thought.

A second text from her mother arrived. 'Hi, Adrianna, Why don't you come over here? I'll meet you in Bayswater. Check my study for an address near the computer. Don't tell Susan or James. Love, Mum.'

Adrianna reread the words without understanding them. She thought about what Mr Dodsworth might have said and his refrain when she set off on deliveries. Read the instructions carefully. Check the map.

She walked into her mother's study and read the piece of paper next to the computer. Mark. The Old Fortune Cookie Restaurant, Bayswater, W2 6LT. Bayswater in London.

She found a travel book on London on the bookshelf. Bayswater, W2 6LT in London was near Queensway station, close to Hyde Park. But who was Mark?

She sent back a text to her mother. 'Mum, I'm coming over. Can I please tell Susan and James about your latest text message?'

After waiting several days and receiving no reply, Adrianna rang Susan to tell her she was going to London.

'Do you really think that's necessary?' asked Susan. 'James has worked out from her credit card purchases that she's shopped at a bookstore in Bayswater and the deli at Marks and Spencer in Knightsbridge. Sounds like Mum.'

'I'd still like to check she's OK. Mr Dodsworth gave me a small retrenchment payment. I might as well use it to go overseas. Do you mind looking after Marmalade? I can bring him over the day before I leave.'

'I suppose so. He'll entertain the kids – for about two minutes.'

As she packed to go to London, Adrianna thought about the missed call on her mobile the day her mother had left. Instead of calling back, she'd leaned against the counter and watched the late afternoon sun light up motes of dust floating over empty shelves. In the middle of the shop floor stood the last item to be collected – a giant globe of the world, the British Empire painted in red. She'd watched the packers swathe the globe in bubble wrap and winced as they shoved it into a van, slamming the door so hard she wondered if it would survive the trip to London.

She'd meant to call her mother on the tram home but was distracted thinking about the final hours of Dodsworth Maps and Fine Prints: the store window plastered with an advertisement for the shop's replacement – a café with lime-green benches and wi-fi; the fire sale where customers grabbed items they'd been eyeing off for months; Mr Dodsworth walking out and leaving her to lock up.

She'd taken out her mobile, but had ended up studying her reflection in the tram window: pale oval face; brown hair pulled back tight, dark eyes filled with sadness. The tram bell clanged and she'd put her mobile away. Arriving home, she'd called out for her mother, but there'd been no reply. Marmalade had rubbed against her legs and Adrianna had reached down to pat him. She'd switched on the answering machine and learned her mother had left – without warning, just like her father ten years earlier.

Arriving at Heathrow, Adrianna experienced a rush of excitement, as if on the verge of an adventure.

'I've come to find my mother,' she was about to say to the immigration officer who asked about the purpose of her visit. She stopped herself and replied, 'A holiday. I've always wanted to see London.' At least the last bit was true.

When she reached her hotel, she spread out a map of London and checked the route to the Old Fortune Cookie Restaurant. She set off for Bayswater through Hyde Park, a breeze scattering blossoms across her path. Exiting the park, she headed towards Queensway station, which she'd marked on the map. She stopped when she came to a shop with red window frames and a wooden carving of a dragon over the door.

As she entered the restaurant, a young man with a plump cherub-like face and black hair flopping over his eyes, greeted her and led her to a window seat upstairs.

When he brought her the menu, she pulled out a photo from her handbag and showed it to him.

'This is my mother, Delia,' she began, her hand shaking as she passed the photo to him. 'Have you seen her?'

'Yes, very nice lady,' he replied, handing the photo back. 'She comes here with Mr Mark.'

'Do you know how I can contact Mr Mark?'

'Mr Mark, I don't know where he is. I recommend the asparagus and abalone today.'

Returning with her meal, he placed it on the table and ran downstairs. She realised she was hungry and picked up the pair of chopsticks in front of her. The abalone was finely sliced and delicately flavoured, the asparagus bright green and crisp, the white rice glistened in the bowl and the fragrance of the jasmine tea delighted her. She wondered why she'd only ever eaten Chinese food as lukewarm takeaways at the shop.

At the end of her meal, the waiter brought over a plate of quartered orange and a fortune cookie which he put down without stopping. She examined the fortune cookie with its pastry corners folded over like a neat package, opened it and read the piece of paper inside. *You will live a long and rich old age.*

She returned to the restaurant the following day. The same waiter led her to an upstairs table and passed her the menu before dashing away.

'Do you know when Mr Mark is likely to come back here?' she asked when he returned to take her order.

He shook his head and pointed to the menu.

At the end of the meal, he deposited a plate of quartered orange in front of her. She ate an orange quarter and broke the cookie open. *Your luck will change soon.*

Her phone beeped and a text message lit up the screen. 'Hi there, Adrianna. Glad you've arrived. We'll meet soon. Love, Mum.'

Adrianna rang her mother's mobile but there was no answer.

In the days that followed, Adrianna sat at the table upstairs waiting for Mr Mark and her mother to arrive.

When days slipped into weeks, she decided to widen her search. She shopped at the deli at Marks and Spencer in Knightsbridge. She visited museums and art galleries. She watched lovers meet at dusk by the Japanese bridge at Regents Park. She scanned the faces of dog walkers and nannies in Hyde Park whose daily routines she could now set her watch by. Gradually, sitting on the park bench, she began to notice the life of the park – the speckled thrushes flitting between windflowers, and squirrels darting under chestnut trees.

One day tramping through Knightsbridge, she noticed a large red globe in an antiquarian print shop. She checked the name of the shop and recalled she'd corresponded with its owner, Mr Adamson. She peered through the window. A tall, stooped man with steel-rimmed glasses stood behind the counter. She opened the door to the shop.

'Miss Lambeth, how delightful to meet you in person,' exclaimed Mr Adamson when she introduced herself. 'Thank you so much for safely dispatching the globe to us.'

She was surprised that after a brief discussion of maps and prints, he suggested they pop out for afternoon tea at Harrods. Mr Dodsworth would never have asked someone to tea on such a short acquaintance.

'So Charles has shut up shop,' said Mr Adamson, passing her a tray of sandwiches. 'Poor man, overtaken by technology, no doubt. He told me he couldn't even work a fax machine without your help.'

'You knew Mr Dodsworth well?'

'Yes, we went up to Cambridge together. We were both friends of your father.' He paused as she put down her cup, as a look of surprise came over her face. 'Charles never mentioned it? No, I suppose not. He and your father had a falling out.'

'Over Dad's gambling?'

'No,' he replied, frowning as he adjusted the spectacles on his nose. 'As I recall, he derided gambling as a mindless activity.'

Not when he lived with us, she was about to say before Mr Adamson continued talking.

'Charles lost out to your father in the courtship of your mother. Sorry, I've rambled on too much. Eat up. You haven't touched the cake tier yet.'

Later when they parted, he asked her to drop by at the shop the next day. One of the staff was leaving and there was an opening for an assistant. People like Australians, so friendly and cheerful.

Except I'm not, she thought, lying awake in bed that night, mulling over the strangeness of the conversation with Mr Adamson, including the claim that her father wasn't a gambler.

She closed her eyes and opened them a moment later as a service van beeped in the back lane. From the corridor came the sound of suitcase wheels and guests fumbling with keys at their door. It was time to move to somewhere quieter, somewhere more like a home – if she could ever afford to live in London.

She called by at Mr Adamson's shop and accepted the job. The following day she tore off from a lamp post a strip of paper advertising a room for rent with a view of a garden square.

A woman wearing a green velvet jacket, short denim skirt and black tights splattered with glitter answered the door of the flat. Adrianna noticed a bulge beneath the jacket.

'I suppose you've come about the room,' said the woman, patting a kitten crawling out from her jacket.

'I'm thinking of buying a cat. I assume that's OK.'

'As long as I help choose it. Hey, after you bring your gear over, we could swing by the pub and celebrate.'

'Celebrate what?'

'You moving in.'

Autumn mists drifted over the city, drawing Adrianna to the warmth of the Old Fortune Cookie Restaurant, even though she'd stopped looking for her mother there.

One Sunday lunchtime, as she was finishing her meal, she heard the words she'd been waiting for.

'Ah, Mr Mark,' said the waiter. 'Welcome.'

She turned round to see a slim man in his early forties. Stubble on his chin, short black hair, jeans, T-shirt and jacket, a newspaper under his arm.

'We haven't seen you for a long time,' added the waiter.

'No, I've been busy.'

'Business or pleasure?'

'Pleasure. I'm getting married soon.'

'Ah, the fortune cookie never lies.'

Adrianna was still staring at the man when the waiter brought over the dessert of quartered oranges and fortune cookie. She pushed the quartered orange around her plate with a fork, taking occasional glances at the man reading his newspaper. Younger than she'd expected for an acquaintance of her mother. Her heart raced as she tossed up whether to talk to him or wait to see if her mother arrived. She decided to wait outside to waylay her mother as she arrived at the restaurant. Shoving the fortune cookie into her handbag, she paid her bill and left the restaurant.

No one stopped moving in London, she thought, as people surged past her on the pavement. She checked her watch. She'd been waiting an hour. Mr Mark must be lingering over his food, or chatting to the waiter, or waiting for her mother.

A woman walked up to her. Straggly hair, a front tooth missing. 'Got a spare pound, luv?'

When Adrianna reached into her handbag to give her some coins, the fortune cookie fell onto the pavement.

'That's too hard for me teeth,' laughed the woman. 'What's inside?' she asked, picking it up and breaking it open. 'Oh, it says someone close to you will return to your life. Thanks, luv, that'll be me son.'

'I have to go,' said Adrianna, spotting Mr Mark coming out of the restaurant and walking past her.

Suddenly she was behind him, struggling in the crowds to reach him as he walked briskly towards Hyde Park. She followed and closed the gap. Dodging joggers and cyclists, she entered the park and called out his name.

He turned and stopped. Grey eyes, cool, expectant.

'I'm Delia's daughter –' she began.

'Ah, Adrianna.'

'Where's my mother?'

He stared at her without replying.

'I've been looking for her every day since I came to London,' Adrianna continued, her voice rising so much that a couple walking by turned round to look at her. 'Where is she?'

'Sit down,' he said, gesturing towards a bench.

As they took a seat, Adrianna leaned towards him, waiting for him to talk. He stared ahead, as if fixing his concentration on something in the distance. She looked over to a pavilion near the river and wondered if her mother was waiting for him there. It was a few moments before he spoke.

'What was the worst thing for your mother about your father leaving?'

Adrianna sat staring at a leaf floating to the ground. A girl and her father rode by on bicycles. She remembered the hole in her life and the bewildered look on her mother's face after her father had left. 'Not knowing why he disappeared. That was the worst thing.'

'She decided to find out, to search for him in London because they'd both lived here before migrating to Australia. She and I met during one of her trips – the only diners at the restaurant who sat by themselves. A waiter introduced us.'

'Why didn't she tell me she was looking for Dad? And why leave this time without telling me, without warning? Why hasn't she let me meet her? Why has she left me dangling?'

Mark stroked his chin, as if considering her questions one by one. 'She wanted to find your father before she told you anything about her search. It took longer than she thought to find him. She had to persuade a mutual friend to reveal where he lived.'

'Why would I want to see my father after he'd walked out on us?'

'There's something about him you need to know, but you need to hear it from him, not me.'

Adrianna stopped at a two-storey house with a pink-flowering clematis vine over the porch.

A woman about her age came to the door. Dark-eyed, hair pulled back from her forehead, a mirror image of herself. 'Dad's in the garden. I'll show you through.' Registering the puzzlement on Adrianna's face, she added, 'Sorry, I'm Jane, his daughter.'

'But that's not possible,' Adrianna was about to reply, but the woman was already leading her down the hall.

They walked into a lounge room furnished with flowers on side tables. Her father stood up, walked towards her and embraced her. Jane excused herself to make tea.

'Extraordinary you're here. Impossible to believe,' he began, his voice wavering. He was no longer as slim and debonair as she remembered him. The black hair slicked back from the forehead had relaxed into a mop of rumpled grey curls. He motioned her to sit down.

They sat and stared at each other without speaking for some time. Jane returned carrying a tray with a pot of tea. How strange to see her father ensconced in such domesticity.

He began to tell Jane about Adrianna's achievements. Adrianna wondered if she was living through a bizarre piece of theatre. She stood up to leave, then stopped herself. She would have to endure the meeting if she was to meet her mother. She sat down and stood up again.

'Are you leaving?' asked Jane.

'Just the loo, please.'

In the bathroom, she splashed cold water on her face and took a breath.

Jane was waiting in the hallway when she emerged. 'He has missed you so much. He rang Mr Dodsworth every month even though they didn't get on, just to find out about you. He loved you so much.'

'Then why did he leave after gambling all our money away?'

'He never gambled,' said Jane, shaking her head. 'I know because I used to meet him at the Flemington racecourse every Saturday. He never laid a bet on a horse.'

'You lived in Melbourne? You saw him at the races?'

'Yes, we lived close by. The racetrack was where he gave us our allowance.'

'Allowance for what?'

'For me and my family.'

'But I don't understand. Who are you?'

'I'm your half-sister. Dad kept two families in Melbourne. We knew about your family, but you didn't know about us. When my mother died, Dad left your family to support us. He brought my brother and me to England so no one would find out about us.'

They stood facing each other in the hall.

'I have to go,' said Adrianna, walking towards the door. Her hands shook as she turned the knob.

'You don't want to say goodbye to Dad?'

'Not now.'

'It's so wonderful to meet you at last. Come again, please.'

Shortly after, Adrianna rang Mark.

'So you understand everything then?' he asked.

'I doubt I'll ever understand it,' she replied, struggling to control her voice. 'When can I see Mum?'

After she'd finished talking to Mark, Adrianna stared out the window at the garden square below. A girl sat alone on a bench while an older girl and boy chased each other around a giant chestnut tree.

She closed the curtains and set off to meet her mother.

Lunch With a View

Perhaps the waiter didn't like the look of me. 'Do you have a reservation?' he asked, casting an eye over my cargo pants and T-shirt.

'Yeah, but I was in a hurry so I ended up here.'

'No, I'm sorry, we don't have a reservation,' said a voice from behind.

I turned round to see a portly man wearing a pinstriped suit. I realised it was Richard, the man who'd shared a few wild years with my sister Selena in Melbourne a long time ago.

'We'd like a window seat, please,' he said, handing his umbrella over to the waiter.

'Certainly, sir,' replied the waiter. 'I'll see what's available.'

'People here don't always appreciate colonial humour, Jack,' he commented as the waiter ushered us towards a table. 'The view here's breathtaking, isn't it?' he added, taking a seat. 'There's even a glimpse of Marble Arch.'

I studied the skyline. Nelson's Column towered before us; steeples and domes sparkled after morning rain. In the distance, skyscrapers shimmered like mirrors.

'I recommend the Coquilles St Jacques accompanied by the pinot gris from Alsace,' Richard announced, reading from the chef's specials on the wall. 'I sampled several pinot gris at a business forum in Ribeauvillé recently – this one is particularly fine, light and fruity, with a touch of spice.'

I nodded, quickly calculating the amount of cash I had in my pockets. 'Sounds like a cool work trip,' I said as he summoned the waiter.

'Oh, no one bothered pretending it was about work.'

I feigned a low chuckle, as if I'd experienced the same thing. I was still working out how to broach what I wanted to talk to him about.

'So what brings you to London?' he asked after he'd ordered our meal, including dessert, which he also chose.

'I scored a gig over here.'

'So you're still tagging along after heavy metal groups?'

'No, I left that behind with the eighties. I work with rap artists now.'

'One must move with the times.'

I took a slow breath, before replying. 'Yes, but sometimes the past catches up unexpectedly.'

He leaned back his chair and raised one eyebrow slightly. 'Is there anything in particular you wish to discuss with me?'

'Selena asked me to talk to you.'

He coloured a little, lifted the glass to his lips and took a sip.

I waited a moment before continuing. 'Ashleigh wants to know who her father is. She wants to talk to him. Selena thinks maybe you could set up some sort of contact with Ashleigh and talk to her on Skype or Facebook.'

'I'm afraid Selena is mistaken if she thinks I wish to establish contact with Ashleigh,' he replied, his voice growing cold and distant. 'I have a family now, and my position to consider.'

'A position to consider? What about your daughter? Do you ever consider her?'

He didn't reply straight away and I noticed his neck was reddening against his blue and white striped shirt. He spoke in a deliberate voice, enunciating each syllable as if talking to a child who'd misbehaved. 'The matter was settled long ago. The allowance for Ashleigh is more than generous. It came with an agreement. There was to be no contact.'

He paused as the waiter approached carrying two large white plates with scallops in their shells. 'That is the end of the matter,' he announced after the waiter had left.

Neither of us spoke for the rest of the meal beyond Richard

commenting that the crème brûlée should have been served warm. I stared out the window, wondering if there was anything else I could say before we left the restaurant.

We were close to finishing dessert when his phone rang. He excused himself and walked out to the balcony of the restaurant to take the call. I stared at him pacing the balcony against a landscape of church spires and grand monuments. He'd mentioned to me during the course of the meal that he had an apartment with a view of the Thames. I thought about where I stayed in Melbourne whenever I had a gig: City Palms, a two-storey red-brick building with white window frames, a relic of the 1960s, hemmed in by tall apartment buildings in an inner-city suburb. It struck me that talking about City Palms might be a way to reopen the topic of Ashleigh.

He returned from his phone call distracted. 'Sorry. Where were we?'

'You were talking about accommodation when you have to stay overnight in the city. I was about to tell you that when I go to Melbourne for work, I stay in a motel called City Palms. It would have been quite flash once with the two palm trees out the front and a table tennis room – you know, the sort of place our parents holidayed at.'

He frowned at the suggestion that his parents and mine might have had something in common beyond knowing each other through the local tennis club.

'The people staying there are a mixed bunch,' I continued, 'mainly contract workers, backpackers or grey nomads. It's close to the city centre, which I loathe.'

'Yes, I remember, you grew up on a farm,' he replied, glancing around the room as if trying to catch the waiter's eye.

'When I wake up at City Palms, all I hear is mynah birds cheeping and trams rumbling by. I think of dawn at Mum and Dad's farm, how the magpies and kookaburras kick the day off.'

'Then why stay at this City Palms place if you dislike it so much?'

'It turns out Lucy lives in the same street.'

'Lucy?'

'My daughter from a spectacularly short-lived relationship. I'm banned from seeing her. Apparently I remind her mother of her unglamorous past.'

'Then get yourself a decent lawyer and demand contact visits.'

'I missed my chance a long time ago. I was wandering round the country taking any job I could get when Lucy was born. I only found out she existed a few years later. A friend who knew Yvonne told me about her. He said Lucy looked like me. Tall as a glass of water. So I contacted Yvonne, Lucy's mother, but it was too late. She'd told Lucy I was dead. Then one day in Melbourne when I was coming out of City Palms on my way to work, I saw Yvonne and a child in school uniform walking ahead of me. I watched them turn the corner and get on a tram. I saw them at the same time the next day. I followed them and caught the same tram. I pulled my cap over my eyes and slouched down in a seat at the back, hoping Yvonne wouldn't recognise me. When they got off the tram, I took a good look at the little girl. My friend was right. She was the image of me right down to the red curly hair.'

I stopped to watch Richard's reaction. He was pushing the dessert bowl in front of him around the table as if he'd heard enough.

I pressed on. 'I try to get as many gigs as I can in Melbourne. I stay at City Palms and catch the same tram every day. Sometimes Yvonne and Lucy are running late and tear down the street and laugh when they leap on the tram. Sometimes they miss the tram and I get on anyway so as not to attract attention.'

'A good lawyer can sort this out,' said Richard, raising his hand in the air to summon the waiter. 'We need to order coffee. I have to go soon.'

He signalled to me not to talk as the waiter came to the table. As soon as he'd ordered coffee, I continued.

'After a few tram trips, I realised Yvonne hadn't recognised me, so I could sit closer and listen in on her and Lucy talking on the tram.

I found out that Lucy loves horses. I heard her talking about a friend taking her to a farm one weekend. It made me think about her riding with me along the river at my parents' farm.'

'Then hire a lawyer to tell the court that, propose that she spend holidays with you at your parents' farm.'

'I can't just bounce into her life like that. It'd be like a ghost turning up.'

'That's the mother's problem. She shouldn't have told Lucy you were dead. A judge would look very unfavourably on that.'

'Stop,' I said, shaking my head. 'I'm only telling you about this so you realise how lucky you are. You can see and talk to your daughter anytime you want to.'

He stared at me and was about to answer when his phone rang. When he took it out of his pocket, I leaned over and knocked it out of his hand. It flew across the floor and landed under a nearby table, where a couple turned round and stared at us, murmuring to each other before turning back. Richard mumbled an apology to them and picked the phone up from the floor.

'Is everything all right, sir?' asked the waiter, approaching the table and glancing across at me.

'Yes, thank you,' replied Richard, returning to the table. He waited until the waiter had left and took a business card from his wallet. 'Here's the phone number of the best family law barrister in Australia. He spent a year in London with our firm. We keep in touch.'

'And in return?'

'What do you mean?'

'There's a catch, isn't there? You'll quietly settle the bill for your lawyer friend if you never hear from Selena and me again.'

'Are you suggesting I'm trying to buy you off? Don't be absurd. I have not the slightest desire to trouble myself with your personal affairs.'

The condescension in his voice was too much for me. I took out my cigarette lighter and set fire to the card. The waiter moved quickly.

In a flash, he appeared at the table and doused the flames with a jug of water. 'Is everything all right, sir? Do I need to call security?'

'No, that won't be necessary, thank you,' said Richard, dabbing the tablecloth with a napkin. 'My friend was rather foolishly playing with a lighter. I do apologise. We're leaving shortly.'

When the bill arrived, he placed a fifty-pound note under his credit card. 'In case there's any damage to the tablecloth,' he told the waiter as he stood up to leave.

I didn't wait as the waiter passed Richard's umbrella to him at the front door. I walked out without looking back.

That night I rang Selena and apologised for my lack of success.

'Don't worry, Jack. You did your best.'

'But I didn't get very far. Richard brushed me off in that smug superior manner of his.'

'Yeah, I remember it well.' There was a pause on the line. 'But you never know with Richard,' she said. 'Sometimes stuff sinks in later.'

Sitting in Hyde Park the next day, I mulled over Selena's words as the sunlight flickered through the leaves of the chestnut trees. A man and his daughter jogged past, yoked by an iPod. I recalled Richard's words about my right to see Lucy. I stood up and walked quickly back to my hotel, rehearsing the words to use when I rang her mother.

The End of Spring

'No one's saying a word,' I whispered, edging towards the other foreigner in the room. Tall, with a black hooded jumper and blond ponytail – easy to spot in the crowd of grey-suited men.

'The Japanese think it's impolite to talk in a smokers' room,' he replied, staring at me with deep-set brown eyes.

'There's not a woman in sight.'

'Look behind you.'

I turned and saw a group of women standing in a glassed-in area with their backs to the men.

'It's not very sociable, is it?'

'The smokers' rooms in shopping malls never are. Try the smoking zone at the east exit of Shinjuku station where the rock groups busk on Friday nights. You can smoke and talk to women there, if you can hear yourself above the music.'

'Thanks. I'm Robert, by the way. You're from Australia?'

'Seems like I haven't lost the accent,' he replied, extending a hand. 'I'm Daniel.'

I came across him the following Friday night in the smoking zone he'd talked about. This time, he wore a suit with his ponytail tucked underneath the collar of his shirt. He was talking on the phone in a fluent colloquial Japanese that I was still striving to achieve. It turned out he'd studied Japanese at a summer school in Sydney after a business management degree, later fine-tuning his language skills with a Japanese girlfriend in Kyoto. He ran two businesses, I learned, as we chatted and smoked: an English language school in Tokyo and a tourist company in Kyoto.

From then on, we went out drinking with the rest of Shinjuku every Friday night. He tended to do most of the talking. After reading tenth-century Japanese poetry all day, I was stuck for conversation, but he didn't seem to mind if I nodded and only occasionally murmured in response. I think he was glad to talk to another Australian. He seemed homesick, not only for his friends and family in Sydney, but also for the bush and the beach. He said the place he missed most was his grandparents' fibro shack on the south coast of New South Wales, and talked about a track to the beach with glimpses of sea through gum trees and burrawang ferns.

Often the last customers to leave the bar, we walked unsteadily through the city streets, arms draped over each other's shoulders, passing office workers leaving buildings with briefcases under their arms. Daniel liked to ruminate about Japanese society and the cultural differences between Australia and Japan. I couldn't add much to his commentary. In fact, I wanted to talk to him about some problems I was having in that area, preferably when sober.

An opportunity came one Sunday morning when he took me to the Rikugien Gardens to view the azaleas there. As we entered the park, the mist began to lift, revealing a canopy of cherry trees arching over ponds and streams.

'The park once belonged to a feudal lord who let everything grow freely,' he told me, pointing to the rambling azalea bushes. 'In other parks, each azalea flower is removed after blooming and the bush nipped back into shape.'

We stopped at a pavilion where a woman in a kimono served us green tea that frothed in wide shallow cups. Daniel took a sip and sighed.

I waited for a few moments before launching into my problem. 'My professor invited me to lunch at his house last Sunday. After lunch, his daughter and I visited Ueno Art Museum. I think it's the closest I've come to going out with a Japanese girl.'

'Don't even think about it. You'd be overstepping the mark to ask her out. You're a subordinate to the professor of the most prestigious university in Japan. You should use the connection in other ways.'

'How's that?'

'You said you couldn't get interviews for your doctorate research. Ask your professor to be an intermediary. If that doesn't work, let me know. There's people I can call in favours from.'

'Thanks, but it still leaves me with the problem that apart from my professor's daughter, I hardly talk to any women. I live in a men's boarding house and the women at university are very traditional and demure. They pick their books up and leave as soon as the lectures end.'

He let out a short laugh. 'When you come to Kyoto, I'll take you to visit my girlfriend, Hanako. She's certainly not traditional. She runs a coffee shop with an interior that pays homage to Western civilisation.'

It took a while to meet Hanako. I had to remind Daniel several times and it wasn't till the following spring that he invited me to Kyoto.

I followed his directions to the coffee shop at the northern edge of the city. There was a softness to the day, with moss clinging to stone lanterns and temple walls. I walked along a street of wooden houses with bamboo shutters until I came to a shop wedged between two houses. I stared at the whitewashed walls and lace curtains before checking the address again. When I stepped inside, I could hardly move; the place was crammed with glass display cases of teacups, saucers and plates of English fine bone china that reminded me of my grandmother's home. Cups hung from hooks on wooden crossbeams, with matching saucers and plates on shelves below. In some ways too, it was like my parents' house with the stacks of vinyl records and John Mayall playing in the background. Most of the clients looked as if they were stuck in the 1970s with long hair and beards that had turned grey. One customer in a denim jacket had fallen asleep over a newspaper, a cigarette still burning in the ashtray.

A woman in jeans and a black turtleneck jumper entered the shop. Black beret, shoulder-length hair, and finely arched eyebrows. She placed a bag of baguettes on the counter and looked around the café. When she saw me, her face lit up and she clapped her hands. 'You must be Robert, Daniel's Australian friend,' she said in English. 'I've heard so much about you. I'm Hanako. Please sit down. I'll get you breakfast. Daniel's on his way.'

She bustled around making coffee and toasted sandwiches for me, then walked quickly outside with a watering can, saying she had to tend to the geraniums. A few minutes later, she rushed back inside with Daniel sauntering behind her.

'Welcome,' he said, taking a seat at my table. 'What do you think of Hanako's café?

'It looks like everyone's settled in for the day,' I replied, surveying the customers reading books and newspapers.

'Yes, it's the only café in Kyoto where the owner leaves with the customers dozing at the tables. The last one to go locks up.'

'It must be hard for Hanako to run this place by herself,' I said, watching her flip a pancake at a stove in the corner. 'Her English is very good, by the way.'

'She spent her childhood in England but I prefer to speak to her in Japanese. She has a different personality in English.'

He wouldn't elaborate, so I left it at that.

Hanako had invited me to her parents' house on the following day so I made a mental note to talk to her in Japanese.

When I arrived, a gentleman with a silver-topped cane was walking down the path towards the front gate. As he passed me, he twirled his cane in the air, raised his hat and said, 'Good morning' in English.

Hanako was waiting at the door. She was dressed in a kimono of soft green silk, with sprays of wisteria across the sash. Her hair was swept up, every strand in place,'

I bowed and said good morning. *Ohayoo gozaimasu.*

'*Ohayoo gozaimasu,*' she replied softly and bowed in return.

'Who was the gentleman on the path?' I asked, still speaking in Japanese as I took off my shoes at the entrance.

'My father,' she replied and gave me a quick smile. 'Sometimes he likes to dress as if he's taking a stroll in an English park.'

She led me down a hall lined with Impressionist prints to a room overlooking a garden and signalled me to sit near a low table with a lacquered tray, tea pot and cups. As she poured the tea, she pushed her sleeve back slightly and the tea splashed into the cup with the gentlest of sounds. The delicacy of her movements sent a thrill through me.

'Is there some occasion?' I asked, gesturing towards her attire.

'I'm taking my mother to Shimogamo shrine.'

'Your father isn't coming?'

'No.'

'Perhaps after all those years abroad, visiting shrines doesn't interest him now?'

'Perhaps. Or perhaps he thinks that it's something only women do, especially if they have too much time on their hands.'

An older woman in a kimono slid open the paper screen door and entered the room with soundless steps. I rose and bowed. She returned the bow, then gestured me to sit down. Hanako introduced her mother and to my surprise asked me to accompany her mother and her to Shimogamo shrine.

'Daniel's taking a tour group to Kurama, a hot spring town in the mountains,' she said with a gentle smile. 'I'm sure he'd like you to visit the shrine with us. It's the Hollyhock Festival today.'

'As long as it doesn't rain,' said her mother, shaking her head as she surveyed the tangle of dark cloud moving across the sky. 'Last year it was cancelled.'

'Daniel will send us a text if it's cancelled,' replied Hanako. 'He's always the first foreigner to find out.'

As we entered the grounds of the shrine, the sun broke through the clouds and glinted through the leaves of the maple trees. We stopped to watch dragonflies hovering over a stream then took our places in reserved seats near the main shrine. As we waited for the pageant to pass by, Hanako pointed to the hollyhock leaves decorating the eaves and recounted the history of the festival. When the procession arrived, she explained the role of each participant: priests in long white robes, mounted archers, ladies in imperial court costumes followed by men holding large paper umbrellas to shade them.

I was entranced, or maybe I was already falling in love with Hanako. Every time she leaned over and whispered in my ear, the fragrance of sandalwood and plum blossom floated in the air.

'You saw the Hollyhock Festival with Hanako,' Daniel said when we met in Tokyo. He made a sound like a chuckle. If there was any jealousy, he hid it well. We were sitting in a backstreet restaurant, sipping beer in a haze of smoke from the grilled yakitori.

Later, he suggested we go to Tennoji temple. When we arrived, I noticed that the cherry trees were covered in thick green leaves although it wasn't long since we'd been there to view the blossoms in moonlight. I needed the seasons to mark the flight of time, I thought, reflecting on the lack of progress with my research.

'The good thing about this temple is that it sits between two cemeteries,' said Daniel, gesturing to the granite headstones shimmering in the moonlight. 'Only the dead enjoy silence in this city.'

I shivered and took a swig of sake. We stretched out on the ground and smoked for a while, the tips of our cigarettes glowing in the dark.

Then he stubbed out his cigarette and sat up abruptly. 'Things aren't going well between Hanako and me.'

'Something's happened?'

'No, but it will. I need you to come to Kyoto on the weekend. Can you make it?'

'Yes, but why?'

'I can't tell you now. When you get to Kyoto, take the Keihan mountain railway line to Kurama station. I'll meet you at the shrine when I've finished with a tourist group. I've booked us into an inn near the hot springs.'

The train to Kurama rattled up a narrow winding track, the leaves of the maple trees brushing against the carriages. At Kurama station, the driver got off the train and transformed himself into the ticket collector. I followed his instructions to Kurama shrine, where Daniel was waiting for me at the entrance.

'What's happening?' I asked. 'Tell me what's going on.'

'We'll talk later,' he replied.

As we walked up the path to the inn, I glimpsed hills of cedar and wisteria growing wild over the tops of cherry trees. But there wasn't time to take in the view; Daniel was striding ahead of me and only slowed down when we came in sight of the inn.

'It looks a bit expensive,' I said, staring at the white villa with its tall stone lanterns and raked white gravel.

'It's on me,' he said, putting an arm round my shoulder. 'Let's take a bath before dinner.'

Bathing in the hot spring, I wiped away the steam on my glasses and took in the view of bamboo and camellia trees. Daniel lay floating on his back with the water steaming and gurgling around him. After our bath, I put on a cotton kimono and stretched out on the tatami floor. Daniel stood at the window, smoking a cigarette, his face less strained than before. For a moment, I wondered if he'd resolved his problem.

We were sitting at the outdoor restaurant, waiting for our meal. Paper lanterns illuminated the river tripping down the mountain over smooth-topped stones. Daniel poured himself tea, took a sip, then put down his cup. I struggled to comprehend what followed.

'Time's up for Hanako and me,' he said.

'What do you mean, time's up?'

'Her father says she has to sell her coffee shop.'

'I'm not surprised. But how does that affect you and her?'

'The next thing is that he'll want her to settle down. It won't be long before he'll hire a go-between so she can marry into an established family in Kyoto.'

'That sort of thing still goes on, even now?'

'Yes, even now.'

'I thought her family had lived in England.'

'That doesn't mean they want their daughter to marry a foreigner. They've never really accepted me – I belonged to a window of freedom for Hanako, between university and marriage.'

'Has she talked to you about her future?'

'That's what worries me. She's said nothing. She can't see what's going to happen next.'

We sat for a while without speaking. From deep in the mountains, a cuckoo called, high clear notes melting into the darkness. Daniel lit a cigarette while I waited for him to continue.

'I've made my decision. I'm leaving Japan.'

'When?'

'I've booked a plane to Australia tomorrow. And you're going to explain to Hanako why I'm leaving.'

'Why can't you tell her face to face? Why do you want me to tell her?'

'I don't want any scenes. She trusts you and you can explain it the way I want.'

'Which is?'

'You're to tell her that I've tired of Japan. Put it like this: when I arrived and walked around Shinjuku, I felt the excitement in the air, the buzz was like electricity shooting through me. But now it's gone and I can't recapture that first moment of exhilaration. I've tried to but I can't.'

'But that's nonsense. I can't lie to her like that.'

'You have to, for her sake. You have to help me. Find some other words to tell her if you like.'

'Why can't you stay and fight? Persuade her to defy her parents?'

'I don't want her to live a half-life between two cultures, her parents rejecting her, along with the rest of her family.'

'That's up to her to decide, not you. In any case, Japan's changing. People would accept you and Hanako as a couple.'

'Yes, but not her family – they're not the customers in her coffee shop. You have to tell her tomorrow.'

Our food arrived but I couldn't pick up my chopsticks.

'Eat,' he said. 'The wild duck's a specialty of the region.'

'I won't tell her. I won't deliver your message.'

'What about the favours you owe me? The doors I've opened for you? I can soon shut them.'

'That's not like you. You've never been malicious like that.'

'I am now. You'll tell her. You'll go back to Kyoto tomorrow and tell her.'

Hanako's mother bowed and then whispered something to her before leaving us in the room overlooking the garden.

'I can't talk for long,' said Hanako in a stiff voice. 'A photographer's coming soon, for my *omiai* photos.

'You're going through an arranged marriage?'

'It's the first step. I should have told Daniel but I don't have the courage.'

'Are your parents behind this?'

'Of course. But it's more than that.' She paused for a moment and looked out at the garden. 'Daniel has no certainty in his life.'

'He runs a couple of businesses. The rest of the time he devotes himself to you.'

'He spends too much time with me. He splits his time between each business and builds up neither properly. But that's not the only reason.'

'What else?'

'He's like a wandering bird. Where are his family?'

'Have you asked him?'

'Yes. He says they live in Sydney but he doesn't talk to me about them. Do you see what I mean? I need someone who's grounded. You'll tell him I want to end our relationship?'

'No,' I said, shaking my head. 'It's up to you to tell him. I'm not sure I believe you anyway.'

'Tell him it's due to family pressure. He'll believe that and it's half the truth. Even I don't understand my feelings.'

'But you've kept them to yourself until now. I don't know what to tell him. I don't understand you.'

'You must tell him what you think best, then, as soon as you see him.'

Daniel would have left Japan by now, I reflected. I'd probably never hear from him again. He'd cut me adrift along with other memories of Japan, believing he'd sacrificed his love of Hanako for her future. But I shook my head, still not knowing what to say.

'As soon as you see him,' Hanako repeated, leading me out of the room, 'you must pass on my message.'

'I think you've underestimated him,' I said, following her to the front door. It was all I could think of.

I was putting my shoes on when I remembered a conversation I'd had with Daniel. We'd been wandering through the grounds of a shrine when we came across two wedding parties, one in traditional Japanese dress, the other in Western attire.

I looked at Hanako, who was waiting to open the door. 'Daniel once said something interesting to me about arranged marriages,' I said.

She remained silent. Her face was pale, with a delicate blue vein flickering in the left temple.

'He said that sometimes an arranged marriage turned out badly for a family because the son or daughter were in love with someone they couldn't marry. The first or even a second attempt at an arranged marriage was considered unfortunate but a third failure humiliated the family irrevocably.'

In the background I saw Hanako's mother moving down the hallway followed by a photographer with a tripod.

'Sometimes, when the families exchanged photos during negotiations, the reluctance showed in the face of the prospective bride or bridegroom,' I continued.

'I don't understand what you're saying.'

'Please, tell your mother to wait.'

A few moments later, we stood in the walled courtyard at the front of the house.

'If you still love Daniel, the marriage negotiations will fail and your family will be humiliated.'

'I asked you to deliver a message, not to advise me on my future.'

'I can't be your messenger. And there's something you need to know – Daniel left for Australia today.'

I heard her inhale sharply. 'Why? What's happened?'

'I can't tell you. You have to talk to him yourself. You must talk to him before you make a decision.'

'Where is he now?' she asked. Her hand shook as she pushed a strand of hair away from her eyes.

I thought of Daniel's description of white-tipped waves glimpsed through gum trees. 'I think I know where to find him. I'll take you there.'

She stared at me, her eyebrows raised.

'It's almost summer holidays,' I explained. 'My parents would be happy if I went back to Australia for a visit.'

We turned at the sound of the front door opening. Hanako's mother stood waiting at the entrance.

'I have to go,' said Hanako, moving away.

'Take a close look at the photo taken today. If there's sadness in your eyes, the prospective groom and his family will see it too.'

'Goodbye,' she whispered and bowed.